A long time ago in a galaxy far,
far away. . . .

For my sister, Jennifer, and my brother, Adam, whom I shared many a space adventure with long ago.

–T.D.

The illustrations in this book were rendered in gouache, acrylic, and opaque or semi-opaque watercolour. The sketches were rendered primarily in pencil.

Designed by Tony DiTerlizzi and Jason Wojtowicz

EGMONT

We bring stories to life

First published in Great Britain 2014 by Egmont UK Limited
The Yellow Building, 1 Nicholas Road, London W11 4AN

© 2014 Lucasfilm Ltd. & ™.

ISBN 978 1 4052 7583 5

59304/1

Printed in Singapore

Stay safe online. Any website addresses listed in this book are correct at the time of going to print.
However, Egmont is not responsible for content hosted by third parties. Please be aware that online content can be subject to change and websites can contain content that is unsuitable for children. We advise that all children are supervised when using the internet.

Egmont is passionate about helping to preserve the world's remaining ancient forests. We only use paper from legal and sustainable forest sources.

This book is made from paper certified by the Forest Stewardship Council® (FSC®), an organisation dedicated to promoting responsible management of forest resources. For more information on the FSC, please visit www.fsc.org. To learn more about Egmont's sustainable paper policy, please visit www.egmont.co.uk/ethical

May the Force be with you!

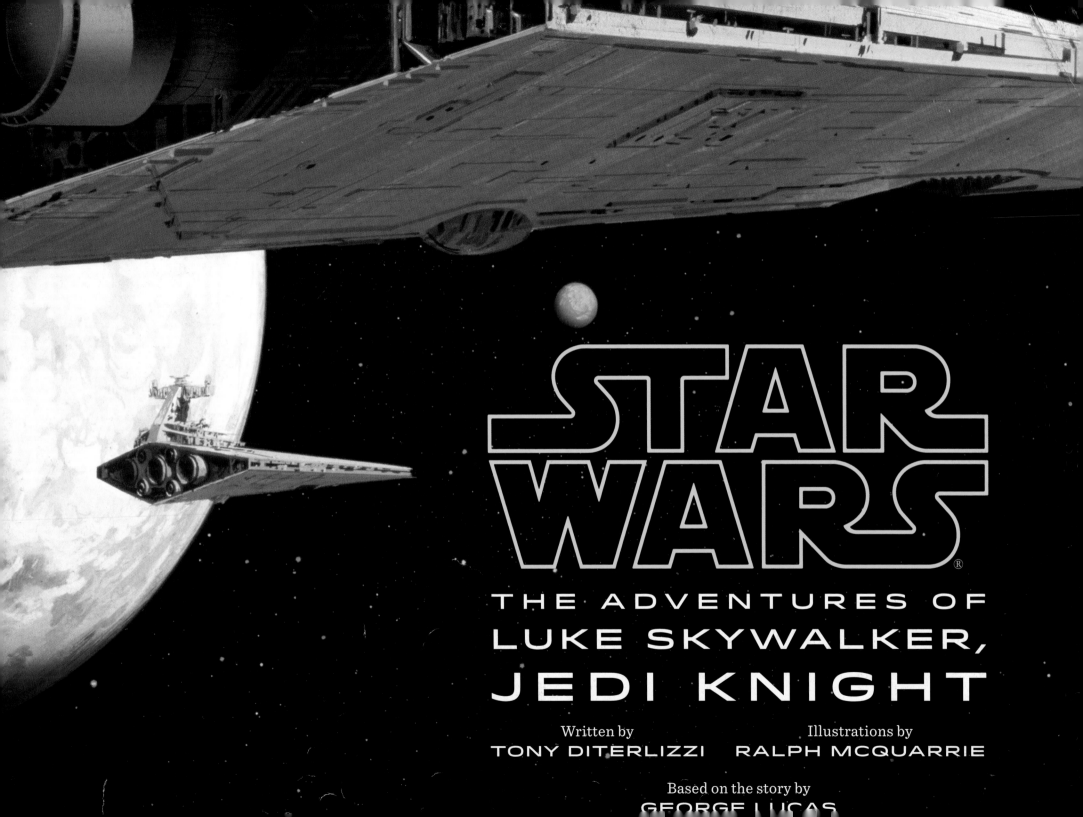

STAR WARS®

THE ADVENTURES OF
LUKE SKYWALKER,
JEDI KNIGHT

Written by
TONY DITERLIZZI

Illustrations by
RALPH MCQUARRIE

Based on the story by
GEORGE LUCAS

This is a story of good versus evil, of light dispelling darkness.

This is a story of hope.

It begins on the distant desert planet of Tatooine with a farm boy named Luke Skywalker.

Luke never knew his parents. He lived with his aunt and uncle on a farm that harvested precious water from the dry desert air. Though busy with his many chores on the moisture farm, Luke was bored. He dreamed of exploring the twinkling frontier of space, beyond the scorching twin suns and his dust bowl home.

Luke Skywalker yearned for adventure.

BOOM!

Far from the moisture farm, an escape pod fell from the sky and crashed in the dunes. Out of the smouldering pod emerged two dinged-up droids. They had come to Tatooine in search of a Jedi Knight – a noble guardian of peace and justice – for whom they'd brought a secret message.

The smaller droid, R2-D2, communicated using electronic chirps, but his companion, C-3PO, spoke eloquently. "We're doomed!" he cried after surveying their surroundings.

The droids wandered through the desert until the dusky twin suns set. With nightfall, they encountered a band of Jawas, grubby scavengers who roamed the desert searching for precious junk to sell and trade.

"Utinni!"

The Jawas squealed with delight as they loaded the captured droids onto their giant sandcrawler.

The Jawas sold R2 and 3PO to Luke's uncle as farmhands. While Luke cleaned the dusty droids, C-3PO recounted how they had served the Rebellion and narrowly escaped an attack by the evil Galactic Empire.

It was known throughout the galaxy that the fearsome Darth Vader was the face of the Empire. Under orders from his Master, Emperor Palpatine, Vader had hunted down and exterminated all members of the ancient order of Jedi Knights . . . except one.

From R2's eye came a flickering image of a girl. Though adorned in the elegant robes of a princess, her face was one of worry. Her recorded voice trembled.

"Help me, Obi-Wan Kenobi. You're my only hope."

Luke knew old Ben Kenobi, the hermit who lived out beyond the dune sea. Could he be the "Obi-Wan" that the princess referred to? Could Ben have the power to rescue a princess and defeat the Empire?

Luke, who longed for adventure, couldn't resist the chance to find out, even though the journey might be dangerous. Little did he know that Imperial stormtroopers had landed on Tatooine. Darth Vader had discovered the missing escape pod from the princess's starship and ordered a squadron to track down the droids and destroy them.

Early in the morning, Luke and the droids set out to find Obi-Wan. As they neared his home, a gang of Tusken Raiders ambushed Luke. The fierce nomads were about to finish him when an eerie howl echoed throughout the canyon walls.

Mroooow!

The Raiders mounted their mighty banthas and fled. A shabby-robed man crept out of a rocky ravine and helped Luke to his feet. Luke recognized his saviour as Ben "Obi-Wan" Kenobi, the man the

Back in his hovel, Obi-Wan revealed that he had once been a Jedi Knight – and that Luke's father had been, too. The old Jedi viewed R2's secret message from the princess, Leia. She had stolen the plans for Darth Vader's new secret weapon and hidden them inside the small droid – plans that would be invaluable to the Rebel Alliance, which was intent on thwarting the evil deeds of the Empire. Obi-Wan stroked his beard, then turned to Luke.

"You must learn the ways of the Force."

Obi-Wan explained that it was the Force that gave a Jedi his power. It was an energy created by all living things. Like good and evil, there were two sides to the Force. Vader had succumbed to the dark side when he destroyed Luke's father, Anakin, the most gifted of all the Jedi Knights.

Confessing that he was too old to rescue the princess, Obi-Wan placed Anakin's battered lightsaber in the farm boy's hand and asked for help.

"I want to learn the ways of the Force and become a Jedi like my father," said Luke.

With the droids in tow, they left for the nearest spaceport in hopes of finding a ship to rescue the captive princess.

"Mos Eisley Spaceport," Obi-Wan announced as they neared the dingy outpost. "You will never find a more wretched hive of scum and villainy. We must be cautious."

Turning down a crowded street, they were stopped by a squad of Imperial stormtroopers, whose white armour gleamed in the midday suns. Luke tried to conceal the worry on his face while a trooper questioned him about R2-D2 and C-3PO. Obi-Wan dismissed the trooper with a wave of his hand.

"These aren't the droids you're looking for."

The trooper nodded and allowed them entrance into Mos Eisley. Luke couldn't believe they had gotten past the checkpoint.

"The Force can have a strong influence on the weak-minded," Obi-Wan advised and led Luke into a noisy cantina bustling with local scoundrels and off-world troublemakers.

Luke didn't have money and he didn't like Captain Solo, but Obi-Wan promised Han a reward once they'd completed their rescue mission. "You guys got yourself a ship," Han replied with a crooked grin. "We'll leave as soon as you're ready. Docking Bay 94."

While everyone prepared for takeoff, Han met with the grotesque gangster Jabba the Hutt. Though Han was in debt to Jabba for a large sum of money, he bargained for more time to pay him back. "Don't disappoint me," Jabba warned as he slithered away.

A snitch informed the stormtroopers that R2-D2 and C-3PO were the droids they'd been searching for. The troopers marched into Docking Bay 94 as everyone scrambled on board the *Falcon*.

BLAM! BLAM! BLAM!

Under a rain of blaster fire, the *Falcon*'s engines roared as it rocketed out of Mos Eisley and away from Tatooine. Once spaceborne, Obi-Wan began to teach Luke about the Force. "Stretch out with your feelings," he instructed as Luke practised with his father's lightsaber.

Before long, they came upon the Empire's secret weapon, a technological terror called the Death Star. This space station was the size of a moon and had enough firepower to obliterate entire planets – anyone who opposed the Emperor would be destroyed.

WHAM! WHAM! WHAM!

An Imperial TIE fighter blasted the *Falcon* while the Death Star's tractor beam dragged the pirate ship into its orbit. The *Falcon*'s controls were useless. There was nothing Han could do.

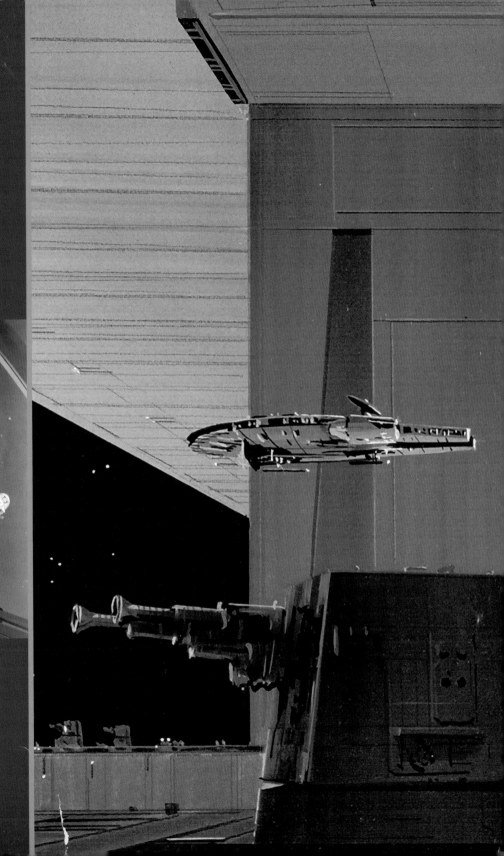

The *Falcon* was forced to land in the main bay of the Death Star. With blasters drawn, a squad of stormtroopers searched the pirate ship, but Luke and his friends were nowhere to be found. Two troopers remained inside the *Falcon* while the rest exited to report to their captain.

WHACK! WHUMP!

The remaining two troopers stepped down from the *Falcon*'s entry ramp – but it was Luke and Han in disguise. With Chewbacca in shackles, the heroes escorted their fake prisoner to the detention level of the space station where the princess was being held.

Meanwhile, Obi-Wan snuck off to deactivate the tractor beam that was preventing the *Falcon* from escaping.

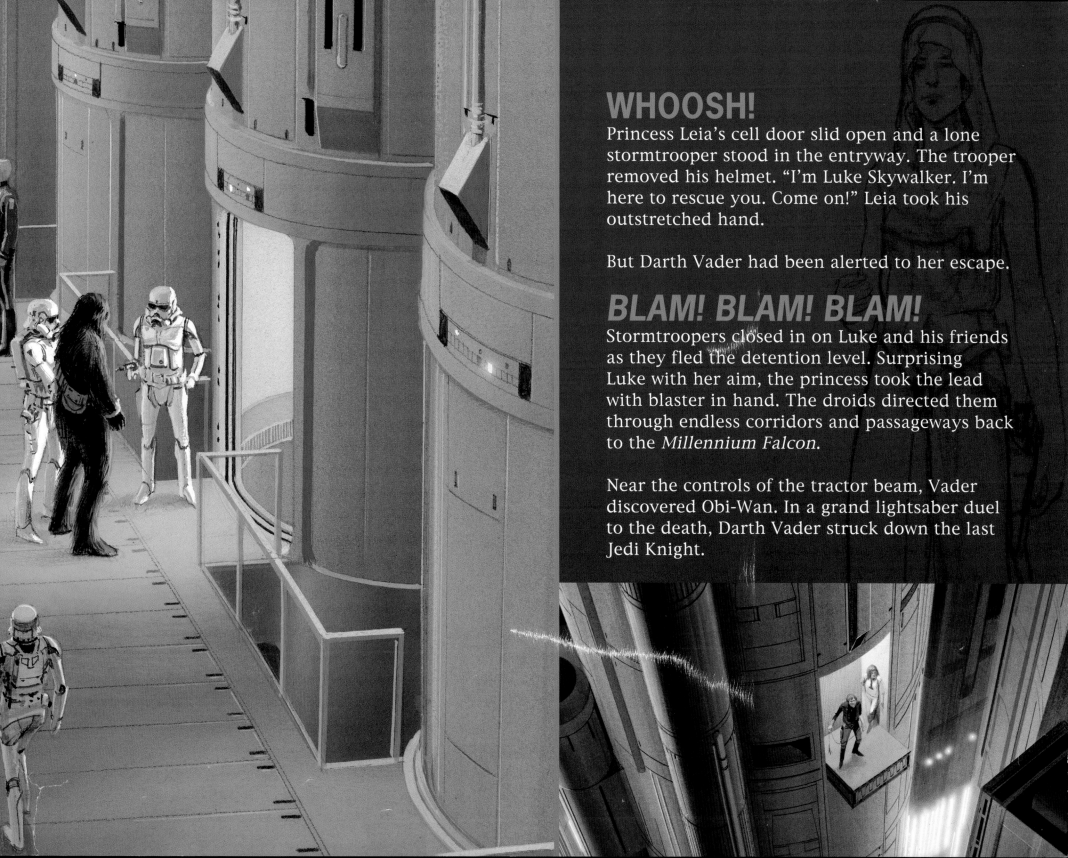

WHOOSH!

Princess Leia's cell door slid open and a lone stormtrooper stood in the entryway. The trooper removed his helmet. "I'm Luke Skywalker. I'm here to rescue you. Come on!" Leia took his outstretched hand.

But Darth Vader had been alerted to her escape.

BLAM! BLAM! BLAM!

Stormtroopers closed in on Luke and his friends as they fled the detention level. Surprising Luke with her aim, the princess took the lead with blaster in hand. The droids directed them through endless corridors and passageways back to the *Millennium Falcon*.

Near the controls of the tractor beam, Vader discovered Obi-Wan. In a grand lightsaber duel to the death, Darth Vader struck down the last Jedi Knight.

With the tractor beam deactivated, the *Falcon* escaped from the Death Star and flew towards planet Yavin, whose lush moon housed the Rebels' hidden base. Despite the success of rescuing Princess Leia, Luke was crestfallen. Obi-Wan was not just a Jedi Knight; he was Luke's teacher and friend.

There was no time for sorrow. Tracking the *Falcon*, Darth Vader had learned the location of the Rebel base. He ordered the Death Star to orbit Yavin. Once in firing range, he would blow up its moon and the Rebel Alliance with it.

R2 displayed the Death Star's plans and a weakness was discovered: a direct torpedo hit in the main exhaust port would destroy the space station. But the port was small. The attack would not be easy.

"All flight troops, man your stations!" A voice boomed over a loudspeaker in the Rebels' main hangar. Pilots boarded their space fighters – all except for Han, who was counting his reward. Luke felt betrayed by Han, but there was no time to lose. He hopped aboard an X-wing fighter and zoomed off to attack the fast-approaching Death Star while Darth Vader's squadron of Imperial TIE fighters prepared to stop them.

The TIE fighters chased Luke's X-wing through narrow trenches, past gun towers, and over the metallic surface of the Death Star. Luke had to hurry to find the exhaust port before it was too late.

WHAM! WHAM! WHAM!

Laser bolts shot at Luke's squadron from every direction. Ships on both sides erupted in fiery explosions. Soon Luke was the only Rebel pilot left. Nervous, he raced towards the main exhaust port at full speed with several TIE fighters close behind.

In moments, the Death Star would be in firing range of the Rebels' hidden base. There would be no one to stop Darth Vader and the Empire if Luke failed. He was alone – one ship against a squadron of Imperial fighters.

BOOM!

The Imperial fighters blew apart as the *Millennium Falcon* fired on them from overhead. "You're all clear, kid," Han's voice came over Luke's headset. "Now let's blow this thing and go home!" The pirate had not forsaken his friend for money after all.

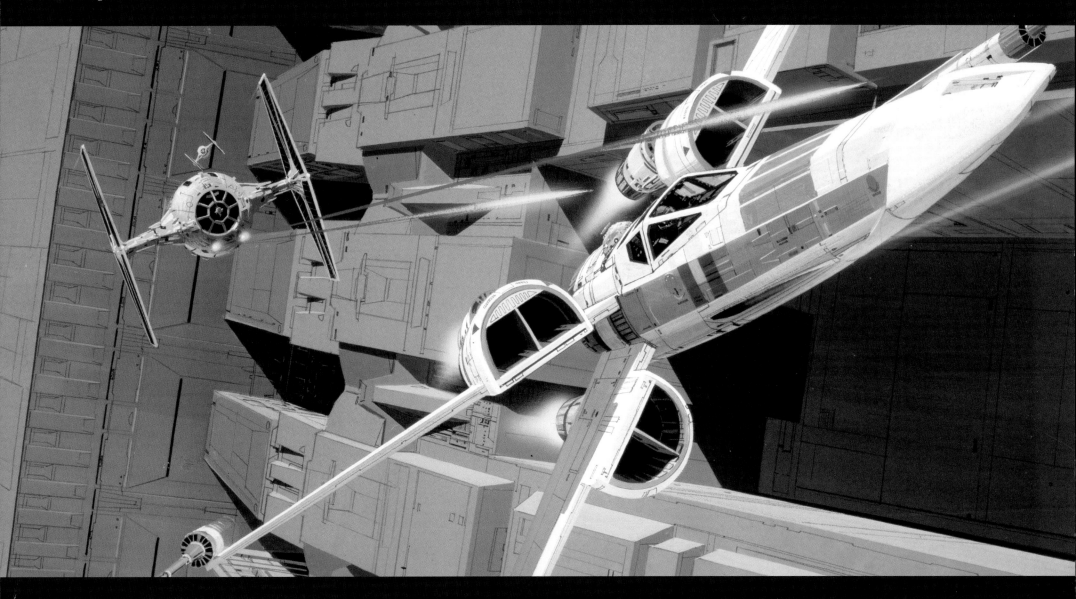

Luke worried he might miss the target. As Obi-Wan had taught him, Luke reached out with his feelings and used the Force. He took a deep breath and fired his torpedoes at the main exhaust port of the Death Star.

KABOOM!

The Death Star exploded into countless sparkling pieces.

"Great shot, kid. That was one in a million!" Han cheered over the headset. Chewbacca roared with joy.

"The Force will be with you . . . always." Obi-Wan's voice drifted into Luke's thoughts. It was as if the old Knight had been there with Luke all along, guiding him.

The remaining Imperial TIE fighters were destroyed. All but one, which slipped away unnoticed.

Arriving back at the Rebel base, Luke and his friends were greeted by a cheering crowd. Princess Leia held a ceremony to honour the brave heroes who had risked their lives to stop Darth Vader – especially the farm boy from Tatooine.

The Emperor was now aware that the gifted pilot who had destroyed the mighty Death Star was the late Anakin Skywalker's son, Luke. The Emperor ordered Darth Vader to locate the Rebels' new hidden base and capture Luke.

Vader sent thousands of Imperial probe droids in all directions of the galaxy searching for signs of the Rebels' secret location. One signaled back an image from the icy planet Hoth.

"That's it," Vader said with delight. "And I'm sure young Skywalker is with them."

From the saddle of his tauntaun, Luke watched that same Imperial probe droid as it signalled from the frigid surface of Hoth. Curious, he urged his mount through blustery snow flurries to investigate. But the tauntaun wouldn't budge. Instead, it brayed and stomped at the frozen ground. "Easy, girl," Luke said as he stroked its shaggy neck.

MROAR!

The large claws of a wampa ice monster swatted Luke from his mount. As the beast began to devour the tauntaun, Luke scrabbled to his feet and ignited his lightsaber.

SWISHHHHH!

In a single deadly move, he cut down the wampa and stumbled away. Dizzy and wounded from the attack, Luke was lost in a blinding snowstorm.

Back at the Rebel base, R2-D2 and C-3PO realized Luke was missing. As night fell, Han saddled up his tauntaun and set off into the dark, howling blizzard to find him. Luke awoke in a medical healing tank back at the base. His friend Han Solo had rescued him.

C-3PO listened to the transmission from the probe droid. He announced, "This signal is not used by the Alliance." Realizing the Empire had located them, the Rebels prepared for battle. While Luke geared up, Han readied the *Falcon* for a visit to Jabba the Hutt so that he could repay his debt.

THUMP! THUMP! THUMP!

The plodding sound of Imperial walkers shook the icy walls of the Rebel base.

Luke and the other pilots manned their small snowspeeders. Their mission: to stop the Imperial invasion while the Rebels evacuated. Luke bid farewell to his friends and sped off to battle Vader's forces once again.

ZAP! ZAP! ZAP!

The Imperial walkers were already in firing range of the Rebel base. A blast struck Luke's snowspeeder. Smoke billowed from the engine as the speeder careened towards a snowbank below.

CRASH!

Luke kicked open the cockpit hatch and clambered out. Scanning the battlefield, a chilly wind stung the scars on his face from the wampa's attack. The ground shook as the walker plodded closer.

With only seconds to escape, Luke reached back into the cockpit and grabbed a magnetic harpoon and a grenade. He leaped out of the way just as the gigantic foot of the walker came down, crushing his snowspeeder. Luke fired the harpoon at the underbelly of the walker and hoisted himself up. Using his lightsaber, he sliced a hole in the walker and tossed in the grenade.

Unclipping himself from the harpoon, Luke dropped down to the soft snow below. The walker continued on its mechanical march.

BOOM!

The sides of the walker exploded, and it toppled in a cloud of smoke and snow. Luke's feeling of triumph was short-lived, however, as there were too many walkers. Imperial stormtroopers overcame the Rebels and invaded their hidden base. The Empire struck back, winning the Battle of Hoth.

Luke fled the icy battlefield and boarded his hidden X-wing fighter where R2 waited for him. As they flew away, Obi-Wan Kenobi's voice drifted into Luke's mind: "You will go to the Dagobah system. There you will learn from Yoda, the Jedi Master who instructed me."

Luke and R2 arrived on the boggy planet of Dagobah. "This seems like a strange place to find a Jedi Master," he confided to his trusty droid while setting up camp. At dusk, a wizened creature appeared from the mists. It was Yoda.

The Jedi Master led Luke to his mud hut for a warm meal. Though Luke was gifted with the Force, Yoda refused to train him. He warned Luke that he was too reckless. Adventure and excitement were not the Jedi way.

The spirit of Obi-Wan appeared and reasoned with the Jedi Master. Yoda agreed after Luke promised to complete his training once they'd started.

Under Yoda's guidance, Luke began the rigorous practice of becoming a Jedi, exercising both body and mind. Often, Master Yoda's requests seemed too difficult. Though frustrated, Luke said he would try. Yoda offered his wisdom:

"Do. Or do not. There is no try."

Jedi training did not only involve becoming adept with a lightsaber. Luke also had to learn the ways of the Force.

Yoda cautioned that anger, fear and aggression led down the path of the dark side. "A Jedi uses the Force for knowledge and defense. Never for attack." Luke had to learn to remain calm even if he felt angry.

As he became stronger with the Force, Luke began to have visions. One of these visions was of Darth Vader. Another foretold the future: Luke saw a city in the clouds. His friends Han, Leia and Chewie were there . . . but they were in pain.

"I have to go," Luke said, forgetting his promise to Master Yoda. "I can help them."

Yoda and Obi-Wan tried to stop Luke. He was not finished with his training. But Luke had made up his mind. "That boy is our last hope," said Obi-Wan as Luke sped off in his X-wing.

"No," said Yoda. "There is another."

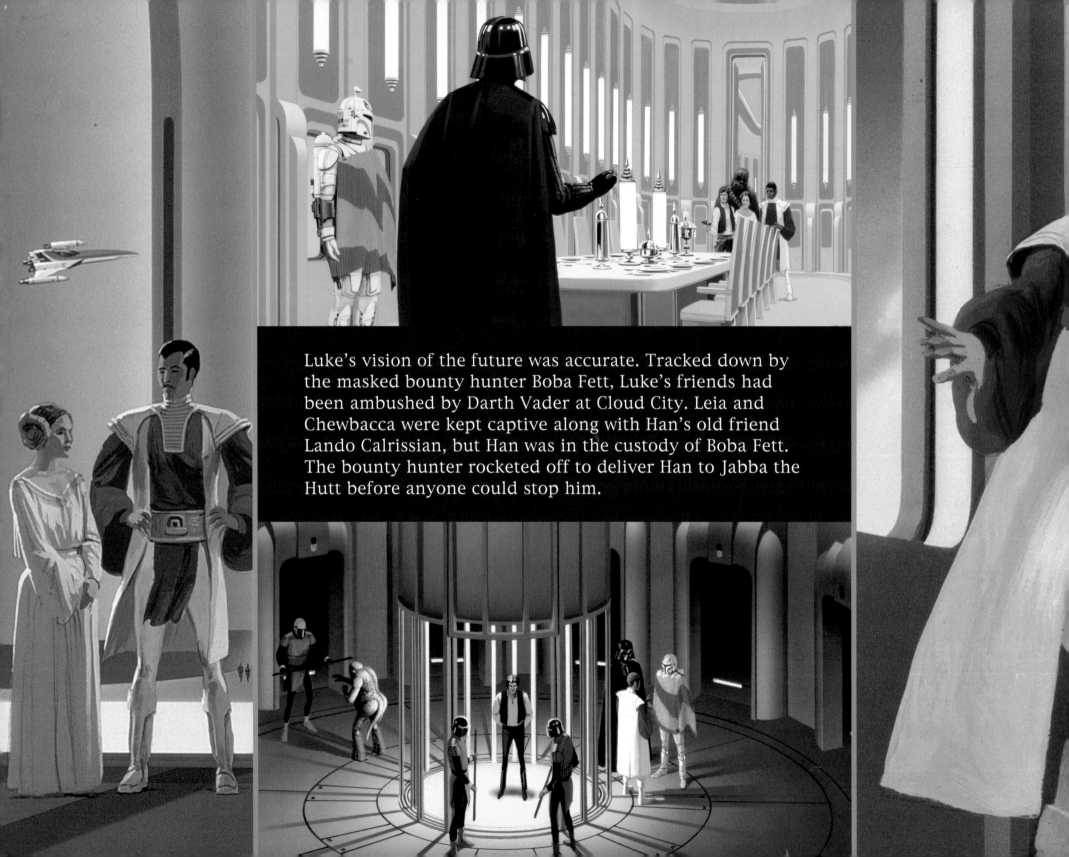

Luke's vision of the future was accurate. Tracked down by the masked bounty hunter Boba Fett, Luke's friends had been ambushed by Darth Vader at Cloud City. Leia and Chewbacca were kept captive along with Han's old friend Lando Calrissian, but Han was in the custody of Boba Fett. The bounty hunter rocketed off to deliver Han to Jabba the Hutt before anyone could stop him.

After racing to Cloud City, Luke set down on an abandoned landing platform. Uneasy, he searched the city's corridors for his friends. He caught a glimpse of Leia and Chewie being escorted by a squad of Imperial stormtroopers. A firefight broke out.

"Luke, don't – it's a trap!"

Leia yelled as she was carried off. Luke bolted after her, but the stormtroopers and their prisoners had disappeared.

Darth Vader stood in the shadows. "The Force is with you, young Skywalker," he hissed, igniting his lightsaber. "But you are not a Jedi yet."

SWISH! CRACK! WHAM!

Glowing lightsabers crackled as they clashed. Luke battled the Dark Lord in the dimly lit bowels of Cloud City.

"Now you will embrace the dark side," Vader gloated as they dueled. "The Emperor will complete your training."

"I'll die first." Luke remained calm as Yoda had taught him.

Angry, Vader used the dark power of the Force to lift and hurl tools and other heavy objects at Luke – who quickly became battered and bruised. "You are beaten. It is useless to resist," said Vader. "You will join me or join Obi-Wan in death!" He slashed at Luke with his lightsaber, driving him onto a gantry that extended into the gigantic reactor shaft in the centre of the city. Shaking with fear, Luke accused the Dark Lord of striking down his father.

"No," replied Vader.

Luke didn't want this to be true, but searching his feelings, he knew it to be so. Vader beckoned. "Join me and we'll rule the galaxy as father and son!"

Luke knew he could never join the dark side. He leaped from the gantry and fell down the reactor shaft to the underside of Cloud City. There he hung from a weather vane for dear life. Vader had wounded Luke with his lightsaber, but more so with the truth.

Struggling to concentrate, Luke used the Force and reached out to Leia as she and his friends fled on the *Millennium Falcon*. Leia felt Luke's cry for help, so they headed back to Cloud City. Chewbacca eased the ship under Luke and Lando pulled him on board. In a flash, they were far away from Vader's clutches.

While Luke recovered from his wounds on the Rebels' medical frigate, his thoughts were of Obi-Wan, Yoda, and his father . . . Darth Vader.

R2-D2 and C-3PO returned to the desert planet of Tatooine. The droids nervously entered the palace of the infamous Jabba the Hutt. There they delivered a message from Luke. He asked Jabba to release his friend Han Solo.

MWAH! HA! HA!

Jabba refused Luke's plea. He would not give Han his freedom.

The next morning, Luke arrived at the palace. With weapons drawn, Jabba's gang surrounded him. Remaining calm, the young Jedi offered to bargain with Jabba for the release of Han.

Jabba scoffed. "There will be no bargain!" A trapdoor opened under Luke and he fell into a dark pit below the throne. Something growled from within the shadows of

ROAR!

From under a large opened gate stomped Jabba's pet, a monstrous rancor. It seized a palace guard who had fallen into the pit with Luke.

SLURP!

The guard disappeared down the rancor's maw in one gulp. Luke would be next. As the monster's giant claws drew him to its drooling mouth, Luke grabbed a gnawed leg bone from the ground and wedged it between the rancor's jaws. Bellowing, the monster dropped Luke, who bolted through the giant doorway that led to the pen. The rancor followed.

Though it seemed there was no way out, Luke overcame his fear. He spied the controls to the gate that closed off the pen. The moment the monster stepped into the doorway, Luke snatched a skull from the filthy floor and hurled it at the controls to the gate.

SLAM!

The rancor howled as the gate came down and crushed him. Furious, Jabba sentenced Luke and his friends to be thrown into the Pit of Carkoon, nesting place of the all-powerful Sarlacc, where they would slowly be eaten alive.

Hovering in a skiff over an enormous sandy pit, Jabba's guards forced Luke to walk the plank. From below, the twisting tentacles of the hungry Sarlacc slithered up to grab its prey.

"Put him in!" Jabba barked from aboard his luxurious flying sail barge.

Luke was pushed off the plank. Falling to certain death, he conjured the Force. Luke spun midair, grabbed the edge of the plank and catapulted back onto the skiff. He landed in the middle of Jabba's guards with his lightsaber glowing.

SWOOSH! *WHAM!* ZAP!

Jabba's goons scurried from Luke's attack and fell from the skiff into the mouth of the Sarlacc. Luke jumped onto Jabba's sail barge and fought his way to the large deck gun. Firing the sail barge's deck gun at the ship itself, Luke and his friends zoomed away on the skiff as the barge exploded.

Jabba the Hutt's gangster days were over.

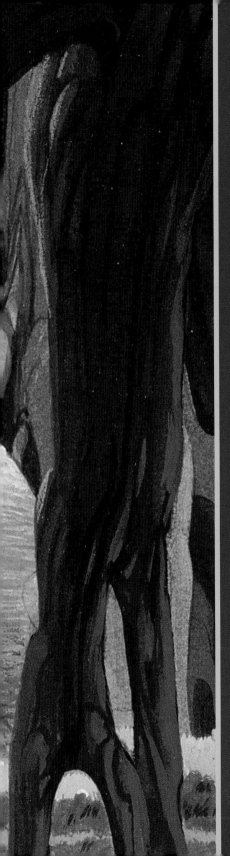

While his friends flew off to rendezvous with the Rebel fleet, Luke steered his X-wing towards Dagobah. He had a promise still to keep.

Now Yoda appeared different to Luke: older and frail. As Luke tucked the ancient Jedi Master into bed, he asked if Darth Vader was indeed his father. Yoda replied,

"Your father he is."

Yoda informed Luke that he could only become a Jedi Knight by defeating his father. With a raspy voice he added that Luke also had a sibling. Yoda closed his wrinkle-lined eyes and exhaled his last breath.

Saddened by the passing of his teacher, Luke was once again visited by the spirit of Obi-Wan. The old Knight revealed that Princess Leia was Luke's twin sister and they had both been hidden from Vader and the Emperor when they were born.

Obi-Wan confessed that Luke was the last hope for the return of the Jedi Knights. It was his destiny to confront Vader one more time.

But Luke refused to strike down his own father. "There is still good in him. I can feel it," he said. The young Jedi fired up his X-wing and left to join his friends at the Rebel fleet.

The Rebel Alliance was larger than ever. Leaders from all over the galaxy banded together in a final effort to defeat the Empire. At the headquarters of the Rebel fleet, Luke learned that Emperor Palpatine had been secretly overseeing the construction of a new Death Star deadlier than the first.

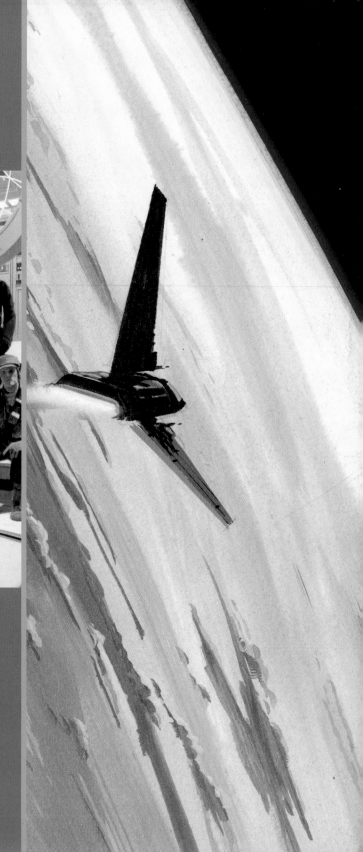

An invisible shield protected this new space station. A generator located on the nearby moon of Endor powered the shield. If Luke and his friends could deactivate the shield, then the Rebel fighters could strike, destroying the Death Star and the Emperor with it.

With Han and Chewie piloting a stolen Imperial shuttle, Luke, Leia, the droids, and the team of Rebels slipped past the new Death Star and touched down on the forested moon of Endor.

Upon landing, the Rebels were captured by a band of Ewoks, the primitive natives of Endor. Though small and furry, Ewoks were also feisty and cunning.

At the Ewok village, C-3PO told the story of the battle between the Empire and the Rebellion. The Ewok elders conferred with one another. They knew where the shield generator was hidden and did not want the Empire stationed on their pristine planet. The Ewok tribe vowed to help Luke and his friends.

Despite the excitement of having the aid of the Ewoks, Luke was troubled. He confessed to Leia that Darth Vader was on Endor. Using the Force, Luke could feel Vader's presence – and Vader could feel Luke's. Therefore, Luke was endangering the mission to shut down the Death Star's shield. Leia wondered how it was that Luke felt this connection to Vader. He revealed that Darth Vader was his father.

"The Force is strong in my family. My father has it . . . I have it . . . and my sister has it," Luke added.

"I know," Leia said, hugging Luke. "Somehow I've always known."

But Vader did not know about Leia. Luke kissed his sister goodbye and sped off to face his destiny, alone.

Allowing Imperial troops to capture him, Luke was brought to his father. Sensing the conflict of good and evil within Darth Vader, Luke asked him to let go of the hate and relinquish the power of the dark side.

"It is too late for me, Son," Vader said. "The Emperor will show you the true nature of the Force. He is your Master now." He escorted Luke to an Imperial shuttle and whisked him up to the orbiting Death Star.

At that moment, the Rebel fleet began its surprise assault on the Empire's new space station.

"Ee chee wa maa!"

Ewok battle cries echoed through the forests of Endor. With spears, clubs, boulders, and logs, they toppled the technological might of the Empire. Along with Han, Chewie, Leia, and the droids, they destroyed the generator, shutting off the power to the shield that protected the Death Star.

Up on the space station, Luke faced Emperor Palpatine at last. The Emperor tried luring the young Jedi to the dark side, but to no avail. Leering at Luke, he ordered the attack on the Rebel fleet.

The Death Star began vaporizing entire Rebel cruisers in one shot. Luke felt pain watching the defeat of his Rebel friends. Anger and hate filled him. Luke Skywalker felt the power of the dark side of the Force. With lightning speed, he ignited his lightsaber and battled Darth Vader once more. Luke's rage fueled his aggression. In no time, Vader lay defeated, though not dead.

"Good!" Palpatine said with a cackle. "Your hate has made you powerful. Now, fulfil your destiny and take your father's place at my side!"

Luke looked down to see his own reflection in his father's black mask.

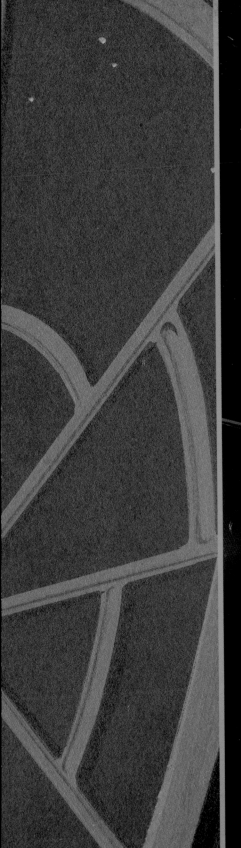

"Never! I'll never turn to the dark side." Luke threw aside his lightsaber.

"I am a Jedi like my father before me."

Furious, Emperor Palpatine conjured the dark power of the Force and struck Luke with bolts of lightning. The young Jedi fell to the floor, writhing in agony.

But Luke's father, who did still have a glimmer of light in his dark existence, could not watch his son be destroyed. With his last bit of strength, Darth Vader seized the Emperor, lifted him high, and thrust him down a shaft that led to the core of the Death Star. Palpatine exploded in a whoosh of dark, hate-filled energy.

On the surface of the Death Star, the Rebels closed in. In minutes the space station would be destroyed. Carrying his battered father, Luke stumbled to an Imperial shuttle.

KA-*BOOM!*
Luke's shuttle rocketed away from the exploding Death Star just in time.

A dying Darth Vader asked his son to remove his helmet and face mask. "You were right about me, Luke," he whispered. "Tell your sister you were right." Anakin Skywalker closed his battle-weary eyes for the last time as Luke said goodbye.

No longer the farm boy from Tatooine, Luke Skywalker fulfilled his destiny. He became a Jedi Knight and saved the galaxy. More important, he saved his father and found his family. The Force was with him.